The Yellow Arrow

VICTOR PELEVIN

THE YELLOW ARROW

Translated from the Russian by Andrew Bromfield

NEW DIRECTIONS

Publisher's Note: Very special thanks are due to Natasha Perova, editor of *Glas:
    New Russian Writing*, for helping make this edition possible.

Translator's Note: The translator expresses his gratitude to Elena Sergeivna
    Gordon for her invaluable contribution to his understanding of Russian
    language, literature, and art, including the present text.

Manufactured in the United States of America
First published clothbound in 1996; first published as New Directions
    Paperbook 845 in 1997
Design by Semadar Megged

Library of Congress Cataloging-in-Publication Data:
Pelevin, Viktor.
[Zhëltaia strela. English.]
The yellow arrow / Victor Pelevin ; translated by Andrew Bromfield.
p. cm.
ISBN 978-0-8112-1355-4 (pbk.)
I. Bromfield, Andrew. II. Title.
PG3485.E38Z3513   1996
891.73'44—dc20   96-773

10 9 8

New Directions Books are published for James Laughlin by
New Directions Publishing Corporation
80 8th Avenue, New York 10011

ANDREI WAS WOKEN BY THE USUAL MORNING noises: cheerful conversation in the toilet line, which already filled the corridor, the desperate crying of a child behind the thin partition wall, and his neighbor's snoring. For several minutes he attempted to struggle against the onset of day, but then the radio came on and began playing music that sounded like it was being poured into the atmosphere from a huge saucepan by some gigantic cook.

"The most important thing," said the invisible speaker right beside his head, "is the mood in which you enter on the new morning. Popular Estonian singer Guna Tamas wishes you a relaxed and joyful day, filled with sunshine."

Andrei swung his legs down on to the floor and

felt for his shoes. Petr Sergeievich was still snoring on the bunk bed opposite. Judging from the energetic heaving of his shoulders and backside under the sheet marked with blue triangular stamps, he intended to spend at least another hour in the embrace of sleep. Petr Sergeievich was clearly impervious to Guna Tamas's morningtime greetings and the voices in the corridor, but his invisible armor was no help to anyone else, and for Andrei the new day had irrevocably begun.

Dressing quickly and drinking down a few mouthfuls of cold tea, he jerked his towel embroidered with a double-headed cock off its hook, picked up the plastic tote bag holding his toiletries, and went out into the corridor. The last person in the toilet line was a bearded Caucasian by the name of Abel—today for some reason his face didn't have its usual affable expression, and even the toothbrush protruding from his fist seemed like a short dagger.

"I'm behind you in line," said Andrei. "I'm just going for a smoke, okay?"

"Don't worry about it," Abel said gloomily.

When the heavy door with the deeply scratched graffiti—"Locomotive are Champs"—and the filthy little window clicked shut behind him, he remembered he'd run out of cigarettes the day before. Fortunately, just behind the door he saw a tumbler-gambler, sitting in the middle of a small group of people. He bummed a "Mainline" from one of them and watched.

The tumbler-gambler was so old and wrinkled, he looked like a half-dead monkey, and an empty beer can for alms would have suited him far better than the three small plastic cups that he moved slowly around a piece of cardboard. Perhaps he was a guru and teacher—his large assistants were certainly very impressive and physically well-endowed: there were two of them, dressed in identical reddish-colored jackets made by Chinese political prisoners from poor quality leather. They argued all too convincingly with each other, pushed each other in the chest and took turns at winning new fifty thousand ruble notes from the tumbler-gambler, who handed them over without saying a word or even looking up.

Andrei moved away and leaned against the wall by the window. The radio had guessed right—it really was a sunny day. As the tumbler-gambler raised his head and his bald patch gleamed in the slanting yellow rays, for a moment his remaining tufts of grey hair were transformed into a glowing halo, and the complex passes he made above the sheet of cardboard seemed like a ritual of some forgotten religion.

"Hey!" said one of the assistants, raising his head. "What's with all the smoke? There's no air left in here as it is."

Andrei didn't answer.

"You deaf?" asked the assistant, drawing himself up to his full height.

Again Andrei said nothing. Any way you looked at it, the assistant was in the wrong—it wasn't his territory.

"I turn and spin, I want to win," the tumbler-gambler suddenly wheezed.

This was obviously a codeword, and the assistant got the message. He tossed his head and went back to arguing with his partner. Andrei took a last drag and threw the butt at their feet.

His turn in the toilet line had just arrived. Abel had disappeared, and the only person in front of Andrei was a woman carrying a baby. They were unexpectedly quick.

Closing the door behind him, Andrei turned on the tap, and glanced at his face in the mirror. In the last five years, he thought, rather than maturing or growing old, it had simply gone out of style, along with flared trousers, transcendental meditation and Fleetwood Mac. The fashion just now was for quite different faces, in the spirit of the pre-war years—an observation which left considerable food for thought. However, Andrei left the thoughts to feed themselves, cleaned his teeth, had a quick wash and went back to his compartment.

Petr Sergeievich was already awake and sitting at the table, scratching himself here and there as he leafed through an old copy of *Route*—Andrei had got it from a gypsy the day before for a can of beer, but hadn't actually read it yet.

"Good morning, Andrei!" said Petr Sergeievich, and pointed at something in the newspaper. "It says here the existence of the abominable snowman can be regarded as proved."

"Good morning, Petr Sergeievich," said Andrei. "It's a load of nonsense. You snored all night again."

"That can't be true. It isn't, is it?"

"Yes, it is."

"Did you try whistling?"

"Of course I did," answered Andrei, "over and over again. A waste of time. As soon as you turn over on your back, you start snoring, and nothing makes the slightest difference. You should tie yourself down so you lie on your side all the time. You know—the way you did last year?"

"I remember," said Petr Sergeievich. "I was younger then. I can't get to sleep like that anymore. What a pain. It's my nerves, Andrei. You know, I never used to snore before these fucking reforms. Never mind, we'll think of something."

"What else do they say?" Andrei asked, nodding at the newspaper.

Petr Sergeievich's thoughts had to be given a definite direction, otherwise he would go on reminiscing about the way things were before the reforms. Petr Sergeievich ran his finger across the greenish page, swearing monotonously as he paraphrased the lead article, and Andrei nodded and asked questions as he began thinking over his plans for the day. First he would go and get breakfast, and then he had to pay a visit to Khan, who had some obscure business to discuss with him.

11

THE RESTAURANT, A LONG NARROW ROOM WITH
a dozen cramped little tables, was still empty, apart
from a smell of burning. Whatever it was that
burned must have already been rotten, Andrei
thought, as he sat in his usual place by the window,
with his back to the cashier. He looked at the menu,
screwing up his eyes against the sun: there was
nothing but millet porridge, tea and Azerbaijanian
cognac. Andrei caught the waiter's eye and nodded.
The waiter gestured as if he was holding something
small—maybe a small glass of something—between
his thumb and finger, and smiled inquiringly.
Andrei shook his head.

Watching the hot sunlight falling on the tablecloth covered with sticky blotches and crumbs,
Andrei was suddenly struck by the thought of what
a genuine tragedy it was for millions of light rays to
set out on their journey from the surface of the sun,
go hurtling through the infinite void of space and

pierce the miles-thick sky of Earth, only to be extinguished in the revolting remains of yesterday's soup. Maybe these yellow arrows slanting in through the window were conscious, hoped for something better—and realized that their hopes were groundless, giving them all the necessary ingredients for suffering.

"Maybe I seem just like one of these yellow arrows falling on the tablecloth to someone," he mused to himself, "and life is nothing but the dirty window that I'm flying through: and here I am falling, falling for God knows how many years already onto the table, right there in front of the plate, while someone looks at the menu and waits for breakfast. . . ."

Andrei looked up at the television in the corner and caught a fleeting glimpse of a face soundlessly mouthing something into three brown microphones. Then the camera swung around and showed two figures jostling furiously at another microphone, clutching each other's identical red ties in a shameless display of Freudian frenzy.

The waiter came over and put his breakfast on the table. Andrei looked into the aluminum bowl at the millet porridge and the blob of melted butter resembling a small sun. He didn't feel like eating, but remembered he wouldn't be back here again before evening, and began stoically swallowing the lukewarm gruel.

The first customers appeared, and the restaurant gradually filled up with the sound of their voices—Andrei had the feeling that the silence hadn't actually been broken, it was simply that a few distracting irritants had been added to it. The silence was as thick and sticky as the porridge in his bowl; it distorted the voices, which sounded jerky and hysterical against its background. At the next table they were talking loudly about abominable snowmen—apparently some crazy old woman had seen one the day before. Andrei tried listening to the conversation for a while, and then gave up.

The seat opposite him was taken by a florid-faced, grey-haired man in a severe black jacket with small silver crosses on the lapels.

"Bon appétit," he said with a smile.

"Give me a break," said Andrei.

"Why so gloomy?" his companion asked in surprise.

"What makes you so merry?"

"I'm not merry," replied the other, "I'm joyful."

"Well, then," said Andrei, "I'm not gloomy, I'm thoughtful. I'm just sitting here meditating."

He finished his porridge, moved his glass of tea closer, and began stirring the sugar. His companion continued to smile. Andrei thought he was about to start speaking again, so he began swirling his spoon faster.

"Of course, thinking, and even sometimes meditating," said his companion, waving his hand like a conductor, "is useful, in fact, very often necessary in life. But everything really depends on where the process originates, so to speak."

"You mean there are different places?" asked Andrei

"Now you're being ironical, but in fact there are. Sometimes a man will try to solve a problem that was solved thousands of years ago, but he simply doesn't know it. Or he doesn't realize that it is his problem."

Andrei finished his tea.

"Maybe," he said, "it really isn't his problem."

"All of us actually have the same problem. It's only our stupid pride that won't allow us to admit it. A person, even a very good one, is always weak if he's alone. He needs support, something that gives his life meaning. He needs to see the reflection of the supreme harmony in everything he does. In what he sees around him day by day."

He pointed at the window. Andrei looked out and saw a forest, and far beyond it, at the very horizon, three huge rust-brown chimneys from some power-station or factory, towering up into the sky. They were so broad they looked like gigantic tumblers. Andrei laughed.

"What's wrong?" asked his companion.

"You know," said Andrei, "I just had this vision of a huge drunken guy with a mouth-organ, tall as the sky, but really stupid and unsteady on his feet. He's playing away at some stupid song, the harmonica's all shiny with grease. And when someone down below notices him, it's called a reflection of the supreme harmony."

His companion frowned.

"You know, there's nothing new in all that," he said. "A hierarchy of demiurges, an incomplete and monstrous world and so on—if the historical parallel interests you. Gnosticism, in a single word. But it will never make you happy, you know."

"I'm sure it won't," said Andrei. "All those frightening words. But what will make me happy?"

"There is only one path to happiness," his companion said authoritatively, scraping his spoon in
his bowl. "To find meaning and beauty in all of this
and submit to the great plan. Real life only begins
after that."

Andrei felt like asking just whose plans one
should submit to, and which of them exactly, but he
thought his companion was sure to answer this
question by forcing some brochure or other on him,
and he kept quiet.

"Maybe you're right," he said, rising from the
table. "Thanks for the conversation. I'm sorry, I'm
always in a bad mood in the morning. I can see
you're a very well-educated man."

"It goes with my job," said his companion.
"Thank you. Please accept this small keepsake."

He held out a small colored brochure. On the
cover was a picture of an improbably pink ear, and
flying into the ear was a twelve-caliber, metal musi-
cal note with wings. It was gleaming brightly—
clearly in reflection of the supreme harmony.
Andrei thanked his companion, stuffed the brochure into his pocket and walked to the door.

He was in no hurry, but he walked quickly all
the same, apologizing every now and then as he

bumped into one of the numerous people who were always wandering along the narrow corridors at this time of day. They were looking out of the windows and smiling, and spots of sunlight quivered on their faces. There was an unusually large number of young but already bloated women in Turkish tracksuits with silent, fidgety children busy with an unsystematic study of the external world. Sometimes, too, they were accompanied by men with their vests hanging over their pants, many holding beer cans in their hands.

Andrei felt that the new day had already swept him up in its current and was forcing him to think about all sorts of things which didn't interest him at all. But there was nothing he could do about it—the voices and sounds from the surrounding space penetrated into his head unhindered and began tumbling around inside there, like the balls in a lottery drum, becoming for the time being his own thoughts. At first everything was filled up with the infernal jingles pouring out of the concealed speakers, then they started forecasting the weather, and Andrei began casting sideways glances at the windows drifting by, beyond which the south wind was supposed to grow stronger. Several times he had to squeeze by groups of people clustered round the traveling altar of one of the tumbler-gamblers—it was really amazing the way all the tumbler-gamblers and their assistants looked the same—they even spoke with the same southern accent, as though they came from a special community whose children all learned the art of squeezing a polystyrene pea under their thumb nail and shuffling three inverted plastic cups around a piece of cardboard. A few minutes later, Andrei finally stopped in front of a door covered in yellow plastic, with the number "XV" and a scratch-mark that looked like an arrow pointing up.

Khan was alone; he was sitting at the table drinking tea and looking out of the window. He was dressed, as usual, in a black tracksuit with the inscription "Angels of California"—which always raised doubts in Andrei's mind about the angels of that particular state. Andrei noticed that Khan had not shaved for a long time, and looked like Toshiro Mifune working his way into a new role, especially since a touch of mongoloid blood gave him the same slanting eyes.

"Hi," said Andrei.

"Hi. Lock the door."

"What if your roommates come back?"

"They won't," said Khan.

The nickel-plated lock made a loud click. For an instant Andrei had a sense of foreboding: the sound of the lock reminded him of the click of a gun-breech. But then suddenly his alarm seemed ridiculous.

"Sit down," said Khan, nodding at the seat opposite him.

Andrei sat down.

"So what's new?" asked Khan.

"Nothing much," said Andrei. "Did you ever wonder where the last five years went?"

"Why five?"

"The exact number doesn't matter," said Andrei. "I said five because I personally remember myself five years ago as being just the same as I am now. Wandering around the place in just the same way, looking things over, thinking the exact same thoughts. Another five years will go by, and everything will be just the same, don't you see? Why are you looking at me like that?"

"Come on," said Khan, "get a grip."

"I didn't think I'd lost my grip."

Khan shook his head.

"Tell me now, quickly," he said, "what is the 'Yellow Arrow'?"

Andrei looked up in surprise.

"That's strange," he said. "Today in the restaurant I was thinking about yellow arrows. Or not really about yellow arrows, more about life. You know, the tablecloth was dirty, and the sunlight was falling on it. I thought . . ."

"Get up."

"What for?"

"Get up, get up," repeated Khan, rising from the table.

Andrei rose to his feet and Khan took him rather roughly by the collar and shook him several times.

"Do you remember what you came here for?" he said.

"Let go of me," said Andrei. "Are you crazy? I just dropped in, that's all."

"Where are we? What can you hear?"

Andrei pulled Khan's hands off his jacket and gave a puzzled frown, then he realized he could hear the regular rhythmic hammering of steel on steel, which had been there all the time, even though he wasn't consciously aware of it.

"What is the 'Yellow Arrow'?" Khan repeated. "Where are we?"

He turned Andrei to face the window, and Andrei saw the tops of the trees hurtling past the window from left to right.

"Well?"

"Hang on," said Andrei, "hang on."

He clutched his head in his hands and sat down on the bunk bed.

"I remember," he said. "The 'Yellow Arrow' is a train traveling toward a ruined bridge. The train we're riding in."

10

"CAN YOU RECALL NOW WHAT HAPPENED TO you?" asked Khan.

"Not very well," said Andrei. "Not in detail. It's as though nothing unusual really happened. I knew what my name was, and which compartment I was from. But it was as if that wasn't me at all. I felt very strange—as though it made some kind of difference which car you rode in. As if everything that happened would make more sense if only the tablecloth in the restaurant were clean. Or if the T.V. showed different faces—you know what I mean?"

"No need to explain," said Khan. "You simply became a passenger for a while."

Andrei turned away from the window and glanced at a panel on the wall of the car lobby, which held two dusty dials and the words "check every . . .".

"I'm a passenger right now," he said. "And so are you."

"A normal passenger never thinks of himself as a passenger," said Khan. "So if you know you're a passenger, you no longer are one. They could never imagine that it's possible to get off this train. Nothing else exists for them, apart from the train."

"And nothing else exists for us apart from the train," Andrei said darkly. "If we don't deceive ourselves, that is."

Khan laughed. "If we don't deceive ourselves," he repeated slowly. "If we don't, we'll only be deceived by others. And anyway, the ability to deceive

what you call 'myself' is a great achievement, because usually that 'self' is what is doing the deceiv-
ing. It doesn't matter in the least whether anything
else exists apart from our train. What matters is that
we can live as though there is something else. As
though it really is possible to get off. That's the only
difference. But if you try to explain that difference
to any of the passengers, they won't understand."

"Have you tried, then?" asked Andrei.

"Yes, I have. They can't even understand that
they're riding in a train."

"It's all nonsense," said Andrei. "Passengers
who don't even realize that they're riding in a
train—people would think you're crazy!"

"They just don't understand. How can they understand something they already know so well?
They don't even hear the sound of the wheels anymore."

"That's true," said Andrei. "I know that myself.
When I went into the restaurant I even thought—
how quiet it is when the place is empty."

"You see! Nice and quiet. You can even hear a
spoon clinking in a glass. Remember, when a man
stops hearing the sound of the wheels and just
wants to keep on moving, he becomes a passenger."

"Nobody asks us whether we want to keep moving," said Andrei. "We can't even remember how we got here. We're traveling along, and that's all there is to it. There's no choice."

"There is, but it's the most difficult thing in life. Riding in a train without being a passenger," said Khan.

The door of the compartment opened and the conductor came in. Andrei recognized his companion from the restaurant—only now he was wearing a uniform cap, and the jacket with the silvery spanners or crossed hammers gleaming on the lapels, now hung open across his protruding belly to reveal a scarlet pullover worn over his black uniform shirt. He was absentmindedly winding around his hand a piece of string with the symbol of his office—a key in the form of a small nickel-plated cylinder with a handle shaped like a cross. It could be used as brass knuckles in encounters with drunken passengers—or as a bottle-opener. The conductor also recognized Andrei. He gave him a broad smile and touched three fingers to the peak of his cap in salute.

"What's he grinning at?" asked Khan, when the conductor moved off down the car.

"Nothing. We got talking in the restaurant. What do I do if it happens again?"

"What?" asked Khan. "You mean with the conductor?"

"No. If I turn into a passenger again."

"You simply have to stop being one, that's all. It happens to all of us."

"What does that mean, all of us? How many of us are there?"

"A lot, I think," said Khan. "There must be a lot, only we don't know each other. There certainly used to be a lot."

"Tell me, who first told you about all this?"

"I don't know," said Khan, "I never saw them."

"What do you mean? How could you learn something from someone you've never seen?"

"That's the way it was," said Khan, and Andrei realized he wasn't going to talk about it.

"But where are they now?" he asked.

"I think they're out there," said Khan, nodding toward the window, which was filled with an endless, drifting expanse of fields overgrown with grass that rippled in waves like water in the wind.

"They're dead?"

"They got off. Some night, when the train stopped, they opened the door and got off."

"Seems to me you're getting things mixed up," said Andrei. "The 'Yellow Arrow' never stops. Everyone knows that."

"Listen," said Khan, "just think for a moment. The passengers don't even know what the train they're riding in is called. They don't even know that they're passengers. So what can they know?"

9

AS SOON AS ANDREI OPENED THE DOOR OF HIS car, he realized that something had happened. Several men in dark suits were standing by the door of one of the compartments: an elderly woman in a black shawl was crying. The radio was not working, but there was depressing music playing on a small tape recorder in the compartment where Abel lived. Andrei went into his own compartment.

"What's happened?" he asked Petr Sergeievich.

"Soskin's died," said Petr Sergeievich, putting down his book. "It's the funeral."

"When did it happen?"

"Last night. They're moving someone from the waiting list into Abel's compartment."

"That's why he was in such a miserable mood," said Andrei. He looked at the book Petr Sergeievich was reading: it was Pasternak's *Early Trains*.

"That's right," said Petr Sergeievich. "Things didn't work out like he wanted. He tried to fix it so his brother could move in. You know the way it is, one greasy wop gets his foot in the door, and then he moves the whole family in. But when the senior conductor took a look at the documents, he said: he's already got a berth in a compartment, and we've got lots in the open cars on the waiting list. Not that I believe he'll actually move anyone in here from an open car. Abel just didn't slip him enough. Or he slipped it to the wrong man, so he was sent packing."

Andrei suddenly remembered he still hadn't bought any cigarettes.

"What's the book about?" he asked.

"About life, I suppose," said Petr Sergeievich.

He returned to his reading.

Andrei went out into the corridor. They were just carrying the body out of the compartment, so he stopped by the window—it wasn't done, pushing your way past a group of mourners. In any case, the ceremony didn't usually drag on for too long.

The pale profile of the dead man appeared in the doorway above the edge of a sheet of plywood held by two conductors. The plywood, which was kept specially for this purpose, was painted red on both sides with a black border, so that it looked like a flag of mourning; for some reason, it had come to be known as the "ashtray."

The body was covered up to the neck with an old scarlet blanket. Abel appeared from somewhere and began struggling to open the window—it wouldn't give, and two other men came to his assistance. Together they pulled the window frame down, opening up a gap of about sixteen inches. At this, the woman in the dark shawl began weeping loudly, and people took her by the arm and led her back into the compartment. The conductors carefully raised the board, pushed its edge out through the window and began to ease the body out—they did everything slowly, in order not to offend anybody's feelings by undue haste. At one point the body almost got stuck, when the blanket on his chest snagged against the frame.

Standing where he was by the window, Andrei could see the dead man's head with its hair flapping wildly in the wind—skimming along nine feet above the embankment, the half-closed eyes stared up at the sky, which was gradually filling up with blue-gray clouds. As it moved out from the yellow wall of the carriage, the head jerked a few times, then began to bend down toward the ground. The scarlet edge of the blanket fluttered past the window, and there was a dull thud. A moment later a pillow and a towel flew past the window: it was a tradition that they were always thrown out after the body.

Andrei could have gone to buy cigarettes now, but he went on standing there, looking out the window. Several seconds went by, then suddenly the green slope came to an end, the hammering of the wheels against the joints in the rails became louder, and the rusty beams of a bridge began to rush past the window as the train crossed the wide blue expanse of an unknown river.

8

THERE WAS MUSIC PLAYING IN THE RESTAURANT, the eternal cassette that always ended suddenly half-way through "Bridge Over Troubled Waters." Andrei spotted his old friend Grisha Strupin at one of the tables, dressed in a fashionable tweed jacket with the winged insignia of the Ministry of Railways pinned to its lapel—that cost a huge amount of money, but Grisha could afford it. When the communists were still in power, he used to do a bit of trade in cigarettes and beer along the corridors of the cars, and now he'd expanded into really big business. Sitting opposite Grisha was a close-cropped foreigner, eating caviar mixed with the boiled buckwheat in his aluminum bowl. Grisha noticed Andrei and beckoned him over, and a moment later Andrei squeezed into the free place beside him. Just recently Grisha had become even more plump and jolly, and his hair was curlier than ever—or perhaps it just seemed that way because he was already a little drunk.

"Cheers," he said. "This is Andrei, a friend from my sinister childhood. And this is Ivan, a friend of my mature years and business partner."

"So the guy's an emigré, come back home again," thought Andrei. They shook hands without speaking. Andrei looked around to see if he could spot any familiar faces. There weren't any, although as usual in the evenings, there were plenty of drunken Finns and Arabs.

"Have a drink?" asked Grisha.

Andrei nodded, and Grish poured three large glasses of "Railroad Special" from the carafe on the table.

"To our business!" said Ivan, raising his glass. He drained it and gave a heavy sigh. "Ah, yes, Grisha, I forgot. There's this big batch of toilet paper, with Saddam Hussein's portrait. It was remaindered when demand fell after the war, and it's real cheap. What would it be worth here?"

"It might be worth a lot," said Grisha, "but I can tell you straight off there's nothing to be made on it. The actual market for toilet paper is very limited—

just the first-class compartments. It's not worth the effort."

"What about the sitting cars and the open cars?" asked Ivan.

"It's never been an item in the sitting cars, and now with inflation the way it is, the open cars are changing to newspapers too."

"All right," said Ivan, "so much for the open cars. But what about the compartments. Or don't the people there . . . ?"

"For the time being, sure," said Grisha. "But it makes no difference to us. I tell you, there's no room there for anyone new to squeeze in."

"Why not?" asked Ivan. "If you're selling cheaper?"

"How can I do that, Ivan? You should spend a bit less time on theory. If I sell just one roll cheaper, they'll chuck me out through the window alive. I tell you, we can't do anything."

"We can't spend all our lives dealing in cigarettes and beer," said Ivan, lighting up a cigarette. "We've got to move on to something bigger. Did you check out the aluminum?"

"Yes," said Grisha. "Seems like it's a real proposition."

"What's the scheme?" asked Ivan.

"Currency-rubles, then currency-currency-currency," said Grisha.

Ivan screwed up his eyes for a moment, as though he was looking at something blindingly bright in the far distance.

"Aha!" he said, then he took a small calculator out of his pocket and became absorbed in juggling figures.

"What kind of scheme is that?" Andrei asked Grisha quietly.

"What a question! You pay the senior conductor, and he writes off the spoons. This guy's serious—he only takes currency. The one condition is you have to break the spoons, because they won't let whole ones past the border lobby, and anyway, they can cause problems. So you need breakers. They take rubles, about ten per cent of what the senior conductor gets. That's the currency-rubles part. Then you have to pay currency another three times—in the staff car, at the border lobby, and protection money."

"And how does he work it out?" whispered Andrei, nodding at Ivan. "How does he know how much to pay everyone?"

"They print the rates every day," said Grisha. "For buying and selling. Don't you know anything? Seems to me like the real world left you behind a long time ago. Still thick with that Khan of yours, are you? Tell me, is that his real name or his nickname?"

"It's his real name," said Andrei. "And if you're interested, his nickname is Brake Handle."

"What's that mean?"

"It's a thing on a boiler," said Andrei, "to let the steam escape. He used to work with boilers."

"God," said Grisha, "a boilerman. You'd be better off making friends with the waiters."

Ivan raised his head.

"It's okay," he said. "Let's go for it. What about the copper?"

"That's not so easy," said Grisha. "In theory it's the same scheme, but all the ashtrays have inventory numbers. You need a separate authorization for each one written off. That means you have to pay the assistant senior conductor on top of everyone else, and I don't have any direct leads on him. I've spoken to one of his secretaries, but he's very cagey. As soon as I mentioned ashtrays, he was out of there like a shot."

"Did you at least run the idea by him?" asked Ivan.

"Not yet. Seems like he's not a player."

"Okay then," said Ivan. "Get started on the spoons tomorrow, and we'll decide about the copper later."

He got up, said goodbye politely, and went toward the door. Grisha watched him go and then turned to Andrei.

"I visited him recently," he said. "Just imagine, only three compartments in the whole car, and a bath in every one. The standard of living . . ."

"What's that mean?" asked Andrei. "The standard of living?"

"Don't be silly, Andrei," Grisha said with a frown. "One thing I can't stand is when you pretend to be stupid. Let's have a few more drinks instead."

"Okay. Only tell me, honestly, aren't you afraid of dealing in ashtrays?"

Grisha was about to open his mouth to reply, but a sudden thought struck him and he half closed his eyes to focus on it. For a few seconds his face was a frozen mask, while his curly hair flapped wildly in the stream of air from the open window.

"No, I'm not afraid, Andrei," he said at last. "And I won't let anything rattle me."

7

"KHAN," SAID ANDREI, "WON'T YOU TELL ME how you could learn something from someone you've never even seen?"

"You don't have to see a man in order to learn something from him. You could get a letter from him."

"Did you get a letter like that?"
Khan nodded.
"Can you show it to me?" asked Andrei.
"I can, but it means a long walk."

The further they went, the more run-down the open sleeping cars became, and the filthier the curtains separating the cramped and crowded bunk sections from the passageway. These places weren't entirely safe even during the morning. Sometimes they had to step over drunks or make way for the ones who hadn't yet tumbled over and fallen asleep. After that came the sitting cars—strangely enough, the air here was cleaner, and the passengers they met also seemed cleaner and more neatly dressed. The men wore faded and patched cotton pants, and the women wore washed-out housecoats; the seats were divided off from each other by homemade screens, and the floor was spread with newspapers covered with playing cards, eggshells and slices of bacon fat.

In one car they were singing songs to guitars in three different places—in fact it sounded like they were all singing the same song, "Train on Fire," only different parts of it at the same time. One group was just beginning, another was finishing, and a third was plowing drunkenly through the chorus, but with the wrong words.

"By the way, about letters," said Khan, as he ducked under one more string of washing. "You've received plenty of them yourself. You could even say you get them every day. And so does everyone else."

"I don't get your meaning," said Andrei. "I personally have never received any letters."

"Have you ever wondered why our train is called the 'Yellow Arrow'?"

"No, I just took your word for it."

"Think about it."

The voices behind the bright-colored curtains gradually changed until they spoke with a distinct southern accent. After a prison car where an armed guard in a padded uniform and cap marched up and down in front of locked doors, they moved on into incredibly crowded sitting cars, a mixture of rubbish dumps and gypsy camps, crawling with dirty gypsy children. And then came the empty cars— they said people used to ride in them once, but now there were only bare bunks scarred by penknife graffiti, and bullet holes and burn marks on the walls. Half of the windows in them were broken, and the holes let in a cold wind. The floors were covered with garbage—old shoes, newspapers and broken bottles. Andrei was just about to ask how much further they had to go, when Khan turned to him and spoke.

"We're almost there," he said, "at the next lobby. So tell me, why is our train called the 'Yellow Arrow'?"

"I don't know," said Andrei. "It's probably something mythological. Perhaps at night, when all the lights are on, from outside it looks like a flying arrow. But then there'd have to be someone who'd seen it from outside and then come back on the train."

"It's not only from the outside that it's like an arrow."

They emerged into the lobby. Khan stepped to the left without speaking and opened a door to reveal the gaping maw of a rusty stove and a curving pipe with a pressure-gauge, on which hung a bone-dry rag. The last cars before the border had been without hot water for a long time, and the stove looked as though it hadn't been lit for maybe ten years, since the very beginning of Recoupling.

"In the corner," said Khan, "on the wall. Light a match."

Andrei squeezed into the dark narrow space and struck a match. There were words scratched on the wall, very old and hard to make out. Written in block capitals, they made up several sentences arranged in a column, like verse:

HE WHO HAS CAST OFF THE WORLD HAS LIKENED
   IT TO YELLOW DUST.
YOUR BODY IS LIKE UNTO A WOUND, AND YOU
   ARE LIKE UNTO A MADMAN.
THIS ENTIRE WORLD IS A YELLOW ARROW WHICH
   HAS PIERCED YOU THROUGH.
THE YELLOW ARROW IS THE TRAIN ON WHICH
   YOU RIDE TOWARD A RUINED BRIDGE.

"Who wrote this?" Andrei asked.

"How should I know?" said Khan.

"But you must have some idea?"

"No," said Khan. "It doesn't matter, anyway. I told you, there are letters all around us—it just takes someone to read them. For instance, the word 'earth' is another letter with the same meaning."

"Why?"

"Think about it. Imagine yourself standing at the window looking out. Houses, kitchen gardens, skeletons, mileposts—in a word, everything the intellectuals call 'kilture.'"

"Culture," Andrei corrected him.

"Yes, and most of this 'kilture' consists of dead bodies mixed up with bottles and bedsheets. In several layers, with grass on the top. This is also called 'earth.' The stuff that bones rot in, and the place where we live are called by the same name. We're all inhabitants of earth. Beings from the next world. You understand me?"

"Yes," said Andrei. "Of course I do. Tell me, did you ever think about where we're traveling from? Where this train started?"

"No," said Khan. "That doesn't particularly interest me. I'm interested in finding out how to get off. You ask the conductors. They'll tell you where the train came from."

"Yes," said Andrei thoughtfully, "they'll do that all right."

"Shall we go back?"

"I'll stay here for a while. I'll catch up with you in five minutes."

When Khan went out, Andrei turned toward the window. It was the first time he'd been in these cars, and now that there was no one around, unusual thoughts came to his mind, thoughts he'd never had in the restaurant, though everything necessary for them to appear was there too.

What he saw when he looked back through the window—a section of embankment relieved by a bush or a tree that was hurtling away into the past—

was the point where he had been a second before, and if the car he was riding in was the last, then there would be nothing at that point except emptiness and branches swaying at both sides of the tracks.

"If everything that existed a moment ago did not disappear," he thought, "then our train and we ourselves would not look like we do. We would be spread out through the air above the sleepers. We would be like a tangled bunch of snakes, surrounded by endless ribbons of plastic, glass and steel. But everything disappears. Every past second disappears, with everything that was in it, and no one knows what he will be like in the next. Or whether he will still be there at all. Or whether God will grow tired of creating one second after another, with everything they contain. Nobody, nobody at all can guarantee that the next second will arrive. And the moment in which we actually live is so short that we cannot even grasp it, all we can do is recall the previous one. But then what actually exists, and what are we?"

Andrei caught sight of his own transparent reflection in the glass, and tried to imagine it disappearing, and another appearing in its place, and so on to infinity.

"I want to get off this train while I am alive. I know this is impossible, but I want to do it, because to want anything else is sheer madness. And I know that the phrase 'I want to get off the train while I am alive' does have a meaning, although the words which make it up have no meaning. I don't even know who I am. Then who will leave this place? And where will he go? Where can I go to, if I don't even know where I am—at the point where I started to think this, or at the point where I finished? And if I tell myself that I am here, where is this 'here'? And what does it mean, 'I tell myself'?"

He looked out of the window again. It was almost dark already. Every now and then, clearly visible in the twilight, white mileposts loomed up at the side of the tracks, looking like small stone sentries.

6

ANDREI OPENED THE LATEST COPY OF *ROUTE* AT the center page, where the most interesting articles usually appeared, under the heading "Rails and Ties." A title in thick print ran right across the top of the page: FUNDAMENTAL ANTHRO-POLOGY.

He settled himself more comfortably, folded the newspaper double and began reading:

"The rhythm of wheels which accompanies each of us throughout life from birth to death is, of course, the most familiar of all sounds. Scientists have calculated that the languages of various peoples contain about twenty thousand imitations of this sound, of which about eighteen thousand belong to dead languages; the majority of these forgotten sound-combinations cannot even be reconstituted because the remaining records are too meager, or as yet undeciphered. However, the imitations that exist in modern languages are, of course, both varied and interesting—some anthropologists regard them as elements of metalanguage, or cultural 'code words,' which allow people to identify their carriage-fellows. The longest of these is the expression used by the pygmies of the Cannabis plateau in Central Africa, which sounds as follows:

'Oo-koo-le-le-oo-koo-la-la-o-be-o-be-o-ba-o-ba'.

"The shortest of these auditory representations is the plosive 'p,' which is used by the inhabitants of the upper reaches of the Amazon. The following is a list of the way wheels sound in various countries of the world:

"In America, 'ginger ale-ginger ale.' In the Baltic countries, 'pa-duba-dam.' In Poland, 'pan-pan.' In Bengal, 'choong-choong.' In Tibet, 'dzog-chen.' In France, 'clicot-clicot.' In the Turkic-language countries of Central Asia, 'bir-sum,' 'bir-som' and 'bir-manat.' In Iran, 'avdal-haladj.' In Iraq, 'jalal-iddi.' In Mongolia, 'ulan-dalai.' (It is interesting to note that in Inner Mongolia, the wheels sound quite different, 'un-gern-khan-khan'). In Afghanistan, 'nakshbandi-nakshbandi.' In Persia, 'beelzebub.' In Ukraine, 'trikh-tararukh.' In Germany,

'vril-schrapp.' In Japan, 'dodeska-zen.' Among
the Australian aborigines, 'tul-up.' Among the
mountain tribes of the Caucasus and, typically,
also among the Basques, 'darlan-bichesyn.' In
North Korea, 'uldu-chu-chkhe.' In South Korea,
'duldu-kvan-um.' In Mexico (especially among
the Ouichotl Indians), 'tonal-nagual.' In Northern
China, 'tsao-tsao-tan-tien.' In Southern China,
'de-i-chan-chan.' In India, 'bhai-ghosh.' In Geor-
gia, 'koba-tsap.' In Israel, 'taki-bats-buber-boom.'
In England, 'click-o-click' (in Scotland, 'gluck-
o-clock'). In Ireland, 'bla-bla.' In Argentina . . ."

Andrei looked down to the very bottom of the
page, at the short paragraph following the long col-
umns of lists:

"But of course, the sound of the wheels is most
beautifully, most movingly imitated in Russia—
'out-there—out-there' (in some remote areas also
'down-there'): the rhythm seems to point the way to
some bright distant dawn stirring us to the very
depths of our souls. . . ."

There was a knock at the door. Andrei auto-
matically grabbed for the handle, and nearly fell off
the toilet seat.

"Will you be much longer?" asked a voice in the corridor.

"I'm just coming," said Andrei, and he crumpled the newspaper into an untidy ball.

"Out-there, out-there," sang the wheels under the filthy wet floor. "Out-there, out-there, out-there, out-there, out-there."

There was a jam-up in the next car because of a funeral. They were letting people past, but the crowd was moving very slowly, and it got stuck for long periods.

"Badasov's died," said a voice somewhere nearby.

Standing in front of Andrei was a fidgety little girl with huge dirty bows in her hair. She was banging her fist on the window as she looked out, turning around every now and then to her mother.

"Ma," she asked suddenly, "what's out there?"

"Out where?" asked her mother.

"Out there," said the girl, and she banged her fist on the window.

"Out there's out there," said her mother with a bright smile.

"Who lives out there?"

"Animals do," said her mother.

"And who else is out there?"

"There are gods and spirits out there," said her mother, "but nobody's ever seen them."

"Don't people live out there?" asked the little girl.

"No," answered her mother, "people don't live out there. People ride in a train."

"Where's best," asked the little girl, "in the train or out there?"

"I don't know," said her mother, "I haven't been out there."

"I want to go out there," said the little girl, and she tapped her finger on the glass.

"Wait for a while," her mother said with a bitter sigh, "you'll be out there soon enough."

The drunken conductors finally won their struggle with the "ashtray," the body thudded onto the ground, bounced and tumbled down the embankment. Out after it flew a cushion, a towel, two red wreaths and a marble paperweight—to judge from all that, the deceased must have been someone important.

"I want to go out there," the little girl wailed to a nonexistent tune, "out there, out there. . . ."

Her mother tugged at her hand, put a finger to her lips and made wild eyes as she nodded at the crowd of mourners. Noticing Andrei watching the little girl, she raised her eyes to his face and arched her brows slightly, as though inviting him to share in her condescending amusement at such childish naïveté.

"Why are you looking at me like that?" Andrei asked the woman. "Maybe I want to go out there too?"

"You mean, to join the abominable snowmen?" she asked.

Andrei recalled the tracks he had seen in the snow outside the window of the restaurant a year before—they were clearly the tracks of shoes, stretching alongside the railway lines for several dozen yards, and then suddenly breaking off, as though the person who made them had vanished into thin air.

5

THE LAMP OVER THE TABLE WAS ON, AND PETR
Sergeievich was smoking his evening cigarette,
dropping the ash nearly into an empty glass. He
always dragged on the cigarette with a slight expression of disgust, as though he was kissing a
woman he no longer loved, but didn't wish to offend by neglecting her.

"They should be put away," he said. "I tell you,
the swines should be put away."

"Who?" asked Andrei.

He was lying on his bunk bed with his hands
behind his head and staring at a black dot that was
crawling across the ceiling.

"All of them," said Petr Sergeievich, for some
reason switching to a whisper. "The entire staff car,
starting with the senior conductor. Just look what's
going on. We got used to having no spoons, okay.
But now it's the ashtrays. Where are the ashtrays,
eh? You tell me that."

"They must have been stolen, I suppose," said Andrei.

"And who stole them?" screeched Petr Sergeievich. "They're not just thieves anymore. We used to have thieves who stole things, but this is a different business altogether. They're selling off the Motherland, that's what."

"Oh, come on," said Andrei. "You weren't born in any ashtray."

"D'you think I'm worried about the spoons and the ashtrays? It's the young girls I feel sorry for, our pure girls, those blue-eyed does who have to sell themselves to all sorts of scum in the open carriages. Understand?"

Andrei said nothing.

"Bare-faced banditry," said Petr Sergeievich in a calmer voice. "They're not afraid of anything. They've got the authorities in their pocket."

"There never was a time when they didn't steal things here," said Andrei. "At least this lot don't throw people out of the windows while they're still alive."

There was a loud knock at the door of the compartment.

"Who is it?" asked Andrei.

"Andrei, it's me," someone shouted on the other side of the door. "Open up quick!"

It was Grisha's voice. Andrei jumped to his feet and opened the door. Grisha slipped inside and immediately locked the door behind him. There was blood on his face and a few patches of it on his jacket. Andrei noticed that the winged insignia of the Ministry of Railways was gone from his lapel, and in its place was a jagged hole.

"What happened?" he asked, sitting Grisha down on the divan.

"I got mugged," said Grisha. "I left the restaurant, on my own, and I was almost home, and then—can you believe it?—it was in the passage between cars. Four of them attacked me. Two in front and two behind. One of the bastards had a sharpened spoon."

"Did they get much?"

"A lot," he said, "don't ask. Ivan settled up today and they took the lot. Bastards. Petty amateurs."

Andrei moistened a cotton towel with water from the carafe and held it out to Grisha.

"Why?" he asked. "Didn't you pay up on time?"

"What's that got to do with it?" said Grisha,

pressing the towel to his temple. "It was just some gang of muggers. Only they don't know who they've come up against. I'll make things hot for everyone around here tomorrow."

"Maybe someone put them up to it?"

"No way," said Grisha. "Apart from Ivan, no body knew a thing about it. And he'd have no reason. I tell you, it was just some gang."

At this point, Petr Sergeievich, who had been discreetly concealing his face behind his newspaper, peeped out and said:

"You see, Andrei, you see? You say they don't throw people out of the windows anymore? Well, they ought to. Just the way they used to—tie their hands and feet and throw them out onto the sleepers head-first. In public. Then we'd have sugar in our tea, and people would behave in the corridor. And no one would dare to touch your friend here."

"And you're not afraid they might throw you out?" Andrei asked.

"Me? What for? I've worked honestly all my life. You just take a walk through the compartment cars—half the doors are fitted with these handles. Whoever's in power, they need me."

"Doors?" said Grisha, suddenly coming to life. "Excuse me, what's your name? Pleased to meet you, Petr Sergeievich. I'm Grigory Strupin, director of the joint venture 'Blue Car'."

Petr Sergeievich shook the hand extended to him, smiled and straightened his collar.

"I apologize for my appearance," said Grisha, smiling broadly with his bloody mouth, and looking askance at his ruined lapel. "An unfortunate incident. At present I just happen to be in need of some professional advice about doors. For a fee, of course—we can draw up a contract later."

"Well, if I can be of assistance . . . ," said Petr Sergeievich.

"Tell me, are the locks on the doors really made of nickel?"

"No," said Petr Sergeievich. "They're only plated with nickel. The locks themselves . . ."

"Listen, Grisha," said Andrei. "You carry on talking here, and I'll take a walk along the corridor to see if there's anybody waiting for you."

He closed the door behind him.

The corridor was deserted. Andrei reached the end and glanced out into the lobby—there was no one there. It was the same at the other end of the car. Returning to the door of his own compartment, he could hear Grisha talking excitedly and Petr Sergeievich humming and hawing evasively. He stood outside the door for a few seconds, and then walked on further along the car. He stopped beside a plexiglas holder on the wall and took out a booklet. On the cover was a portrait of the author, a man with a mustache who looked like a much thinner, wiser and more sober version of Nietzsche, and the booklet was called *A Guide to the Railways of India.* About half the pages were missing, crudely ripped off the staples. Andrei stopped in the well-lit space before the lobby, rested his foot on the triangular lid of the rubbish bin, leaned against the window and began to read the page that would have been next to leave the booklet:

". . . advised by His Reverence Shri Livmilon, I asked myself the question. The answer came almost immediately—all of my conscious life, the thing I have loved most of all is to stand by an open window in the corridor with my arms outside and my foot on the triangular lid of the rubbish bin, watching the wall of the jungle rushing past. Sometimes I have to press my shoulder against the glass to let people through into the lobby, and then I remember that I am standing at the window of a car hurtling across India, but all the rest of the time I am not really aware what is happening and to whom. Have you not noticed, dear reader, that when you look at the world for a long time and forget about yourself, nothing is left except what you see: a low slope covered with thickets of hemp (which people begin to gather with special sticks as soon as the train slows down), a line of palms twined round with lianas, separating the railway from the rest of the world, occasionally a river or a bridge in the colonial style, or an empty road defended by the steel arm of a boom. Where do I go to at such times? And where do these trees and booms go to when nobody is looking at them?

"What does it matter to me? There is something else far more important. I am closest of all to happiness—although I won't attempt to define just what it is—when I turn away from the window and am aware, with the edge of my consciousness, that a moment ago I was not here, there was simply the world outside the window, and something beautiful and incomprehensible, something which there is absolutely no need to 'comprehend,' existed for a few seconds instead of the usual swarm of thoughts, of which one, like a locomotive, pulls all the others after it, absorbs them all and calls itself 'I.' Once again the trumpet call of an elephant in the distance, no doubt a white one—this is happiness. . . ."

"Hey!"

Andrei looked up. Grisha was standing in front of him.

"Well? Did you see anyone?"

"No," Andrei answered. "But you'd better stay in the compartment for another half hour just in case."

"No," said Grisha, "I'll go. Your neighbor turned out to be a pretty useful guy. I've set up a meeting with him for tomorrow. See you."

"See you."

Grisha disappeared behind the door of the lobby. Andrei closed the brochure, stuffed it into his pocket and went back to his compartment.

Five minutes later, when the light was switched off, and Andrei was struggling hard to fall asleep before Petr Sergeievich could begin snoring, Petr Sergeievich unexpectedly cleared his throat and asked:

"Tell me, Andrei, why does Grisha call you a mystic? Is he joking?"

"Yes," said Andrei, "of course he is. He's the biggest mystic we have around here."

4

AS ALWAYS, ANDREI WAS WOKEN BY THE RADIO—a boundless baritone reciting poetry:

"She lies and stares as if still living
From the embankment ditch out there
A lovely girl with colored kerchief
Tied loosely round her braided hair.
The train went rumbling on as usual
Its coaches juddering and creaking,
First class and Second were silent,
Third class was filled with songs and weeping. . . ."

Petr Sergeievich was still snoring. Andrei glanced out of the window. The sky was low and grey, and it was misty with rain—the small drops splattered against the glass.

There was a knock at the door.

"Come in!"

The conductor brought in their tea. He put the glasses on the table, picked up the hundred-ruble note and closed the nickel-plated lock of the door behind him with a click.

The click woke Petr Sergeievich. Instead of turning back to face the wall and go to sleep for another couple of hours as usual, he sprang up and supported himself on his elbow, staring at Andrei with a crazy expression on his face.

"You were snoring again last night," said Andrei.

"Yes? Did you whistle?"

"Of course I did," answered Andrei.

"What time is it?" asked Petr Sergeievich.

"Half past nine."

Petr Sergeievich swore, leapt to his feet and began hastily combing his hair; Andrei now saw that he'd slept in his suit, complete with a tie.

"Where are you off to in such a hurry?" asked Andrei.

"Business," said Petr Sergeievich, shoving under his arm a worn leather briefcase that Andrei hadn't seen him touch for three years, and dashed out into the corridor. Andrei turned to face the wall and closed his eyes. The poetry on the radio was over, and the announcements had begun. Andrei turned the volume control counter-clockwise as far as it would go, but the voices were still clearly audible.

"All of us look forward to a better day," sang a children's choir, "as the Blue Car goes rolling on its way." "The 'Blue Car' company," proclaimed an excited contralto voice in follow-up, "Our train is a real express!"

That was Grisha's advertisement. Then the speaker gave out a squeaking noise, and a jolly male voice announced: "Try a 'Combat' cigarette—it's the greatest feeling yet." Then there was a long pause, followed eventually by "Morning Cinema."

"Today we shall be discussing Japanese director Akira Kurosawa's film *Dodeskaden,*" the announcer said in a nasal voice. "Made in 1970, the film is based on a short novel by Akutagawa Ryūnosuke, *The Rhythm of Invisible Wheels.* In fact, the very title of the film in Japanese is a representation of the sound of wheels hammering against the rails. So close your eyes and imagine it is early morning in a post-war Japanese compartment car. Doors are banging as people hurry out into the corridor on their way to work. The famous sun of Japan is shining brightly outside the windows darkened by the smoke of recent battles. Suddenly, there among the crowd, is the first of the film's heroes, the one who is known in his car as 'the streetcar madman.' This young man imagines that he is the driver of an invisible small train—a 'streetcar' in Japanese—which runs to and fro in the real car. A concept, I'm sure you'll agree, which is far from simple and requires some effort to grasp. . . ."

Andrei got up and began to dress quickly. When he had his jacket on he fastened all the buttons, took his sunglasses and peaked cap down from the upper bunk, and then put the gloves and small wooden wedge he kept under his mattress into his pocket. While he was getting dressed the radio was barely audible, but when he halted for a moment in the doorway, wondering whether he'd taken everything he needed, he heard the insinuating, nasal voice once again:

". . . it must be admitted that the heroes of the film are occupied with genuinely important and serious matters—small-scale wholesale trade, slow death by starvation, theft, childbirth and so forth. And so, in drawing a parallel between the life of these people and the actions of the 'streetcar madman,' who runs up and down the corridor of the carriage, shouting 'dodeska-den! dodeska-den!' in imitation of the rhythm of the wheels of his imaginary train, Kurosawa is, as it were, attempting to show that each of his socially adjusted heroes is in effect traveling around the real carriage in his own little imaginary 'streetcar.' However, Kurosawa fails to indicate any way out of the stark, comfortless world he shows us. What point is there in simply alarming people, and then . . ."

The radio was not on in the corridor.

Andrei was lucky, he only had to go two lobbies in one direction before he found himself in a completely empty corridor. To judge from the smell, they had been poisoning the cockroaches, and the passengers had taken shelter from the odor behind closed doors. Andrei walked quickly along the dusty carpet, and halted beside the door of the service compartment, where the conductor was humming as he hunched over the huge metal sink and washed empty beer cans—in the next car they painted them in a folk-art style and sold them to the West. Andrei waited for a moment when the conductor was looking the other way, slipped past his door and went into the toilet. He locked himself in, forced the wedge between the door and the lever of the lock, and hammered on it several times with his palm—now not even the conductor could open the door from the outside with his key.

The window opened straight away. Andrei glanced through the gap—all the windows nearby were closed. He put on the gloves, the cap and the dark glasses, turned his back to the window and felt with his outstretched hands for the upper rim of the frame. Then he braced his foot against the metal handle on the wall, doubled over and began slowly and cautiously working his way outside.

He knew all the movements so well he could perform them with his eyes closed, but even so every time he had a few moments of anxiety. In the occult books that they sold in the lobby by the restaurant, the procedure was described in a very confused and mysterious fashion, full of allegorical phrases—the books were obviously written by people who didn't really know what they were talking about. The simplest euphemism used for the pro-

cess was the expression 'ritual death.' In a certain
sense it was that—the same thing happened to dead
people who were pushed out of the windows onto
the embankment. But that was the only similarity,
even though the procedure actually was quite risky.
As for the dark subconscious fear, the only means
to combat that were a clear head and a sense of
humor—Andrei reminded himself that he was simply climbing on to the roof of the car.

Above the window there was a hollow gutter to
drain away rain from the roof. Andrei grabbed hold
of its rim and pulled himself up until he was sitting
on the edge of the window with his legs dangling
inside the car. Far ahead, he caught sight of a strip
of green bushes, and he started climbing more
quickly, to avoid being lashed by the branches. A
few seconds later he was up on the ribbed and
strangely wide roof of the car, covered with flaking
yellow paint and punctuated by the rusty protruding
mushrooms of the ventilation turrets. He stood up
and looked around.

A long way to the west there were people standing on the roof, but he couldn't make out any
faces. Andrei jumped over the gaps between several
cars until he found a dent which told him that

he was above Khan's car, and he stamped on the roof.

Khan appeared about five minutes later, wearing an oil-skin jacket with a hood and the same kind of glasses as Andrei. They set off toward the west without speaking, running up to leap over the gaps above the rubber passageways that linked the cars.

Soon they were past the slippery roof of the restaurant and the car with the border-guard lobby, and the people up ahead began to wave their hands in greeting. Andrei recognized several of them and he waved back. He didn't actually know any of them in the usual sense—all communication with the people that he and Khan met up here consisted entirely of an exchange of gestures. They walked past an old man in a dirty padded jacket and an old military fur hat—as usual, he was sitting motionless with his legs crossed in the center of the roof and smoking a long-stemmed pipe with a tiny metal chibouk (it was a mystery how he managed to light it in the wind). Further on there was a group of people sitting in grey cassocks—their faces were hidden by hoods, so it was impossible to tell what age they were, or whether they were men or women.

They sat in a circle, studying an incomprehensible geometrical figure traced on the train roof in charcoal. The figure was the same as it had always been—a circle with a symmetrical design like an open star. Andrei recalled that the previous summer, and the summer before that, they were doing the same thing, but he had no idea what their purpose was in gazing at this simple drawing for so long.

In general, Andrei doubted that the people he met on the roof climbed up there with any particular purpose in mind. He himself had never had any such purpose, and he didn't expect anything from these outings. True, it was here that he first met Khan. That time they hadn't exchanged a word—nobody ever spoke to anybody else up here—but they recognized each other in the corridor a couple of days later. Khan said later that climbing out on to the roof was probably not only pointless, but positively harmful, because it only removed you even further from any real chance of leaving the train—but he still went on climbing up there, simply in order to get away for a while from the stifling communal space of life and death. Neither the beginning nor the end of the train was visible—in both directions the line of carriages extended to the very horizon, curving several times on its way, but nonetheless, somewhere there was a locomotive. Apart from the numerous arguments of metaphysical speculation which went on in the cars below, there were two direct proofs of this—the thick copper cable half a yard above their heads, and the long low rumbling sound that could sometimes be heard from an invisible source.

Andrei felt Khan tug at his sleeve, and then looked where he was pointing. On the roof of the next car there was a rather strange group—four people dressed up like musicians, in exaggerated Latin American costumes. A moment later Andrei noticed the instruments in their hands and realized that they actually were musicians. The clattering of the wheels made it quite impossible to hear the music, but he could see the small orchestra was putting everything they had into it—the one with the pan pipes was squatting down as he played, and the guitarists' faces were so frenzied, they might have been holding rifles instead of guitars. They looked as though they were storming Pablo Escobar's armored carriage. Looking beyond them, Andrei saw a strange figure with a broad-rimmed straw hat hanging at his back—he was standing dangerously close to the edge of the train, dancing on the spot and waving his arms about as though trying to keep warm. Andrei had never come across this man or the musicians up here before.

The train was rushing at speed toward a river, or perhaps a narrow offshoot of a lake, spanned by a strange bridge with very low barriers that barely came up to the roof of the train. The thought occurred to Andrei that you could probably jump over them—and at that very moment the man with the hat on a string pushed off hard from the roof of the train and went flying over the barrier.

For a few seconds, Andrei could not believe it had really happened. Then he dropped onto his belly, crawled to the edge of the roof and hung over it in an attempt to see something. The water under the bridge was practically motionless; there were circles spreading across the surface, and bobbing up and down at their center like a huge water lily was the hat. A few long seconds later a head came bobbing up to the surface like a black ball. The man swam to the water's edge, and then a grassy embankment hid the entire scene from view.

Andrei rose to his feet and looked at Khan. He was shaking his head in admiration and his lips were moving as though he was saying something. Everybody nearby was looking back toward the river they could no longer see—even the incomprehensible group in the cassocks, who usually paid no attention to the others, were standing and gazing, perplexed, toward the east, where the stranger had left them forever. Only the old man in the fur hat carried on sitting motionless in his usual spot, releasing barely visible spurts of smoke into the wind—Andrei couldn't tell whether he simply hadn't noticed anything, or whether he'd seen it all before. The musicians had disappeared. Andrei looked around for them and spotted several small figures jumping from one car to the next, already quite a long way to the horizon.

3

"LIKE IT?" ASKED ANTON. "BE HONEST."

"What?"

"The new series," said Anton, nodding toward the table.

"What series?" asked Andrei. "They're all the same."

"That's the concept," said Anton. "They're numbered, like lithographs."

Andrei was sitting on the edge of the bunk bed, looking at the beer can that Anton was painting. Anton muttered quietly as he traced a small brush over the surface of the can, bending his neck in an unnatural manner in order not to get paint on his beard, but despite this, there were already several white blobs on it, looking like patches of pre- maturely grey hair. Several painted cans stood on the table, all with the same design: the corridor of a car with rosy-cheeked girls in traditional Russian costumes carrying glasses of tea, and flaxen-haired youths in red peasant shirts, all with the same face, like a cow's udder.

"Well?" Anton asked again.

"I think it's good," said Anton. "But there's too much social comment. 'The Lord's Budweiser' was much better."

"I don't understand," said Anton, "why everything I paint has to be compared with the 'Budweiser.'"

"It just came to mind," said Andrei. "It was a really brilliant piece."

Sitting opposite Anton was his wife Olga, who was cleaning down the cans with fine sandpaper. Her legs were covered with a blanket because the door of the compartment had been taken off its hinges, and there was a strong draft across the floor. Another blanket hung in place of the door, but it didn't reach down to the floor, and they could see the shoes and slippers of people walking along the corridor. Andrei looked up at the bent hinges and shook his head.

"I can't understand why you allowed them to take the door down," he said. "Nobody had any right to do it if you didn't agree."

"Nobody asked us if we agreed or not," said

67

Anton. "They just came and told us it was Conversion. From compartments to open cars. They gave us something to sign, and that was that. I don't want to talk about it. Have you seen any of our friends around recently?"

"I see Grisha pretty often," said Andrei. "He's got lots of money now. And I saw Sergei just recently. He's changed a lot. Doesn't drink or smoke. He's become a bedeist."

"What's that?"

"It's a religion, a very beautiful one. They believe we're being pulled along by a 'B.D. 3' locomotive—sometimes they just call it a 'Number 3,' and we're traveling toward a Bright Dawn. Those who believe in the 'B.D. 3' will pass over the final bridge, but the others won't."

"Yes?" said Anton. "That's something I never heard of before. You don't happen to have accepted it, I suppose?"

"No, I haven't," said Andrei. "I haven't changed at all. I'm just reading this interesting little book I came across by accident. It's called *A Guide to the Railways of India*. I can lend it to you when I'm finished, if you like."

"What's it about?" Anton asked, lifting the beer can up over his head and scrutinizing it.

"It's not so easy to describe. It's just this person riding across India in a train and writing about what happens to him. It's not even really clear whether he actually is riding across India or simply imagining it. You'd enjoy it."

"Have you got it with you?" Anton asked.

"Yes," said Andrei.

"Read me a bit, will you? My hands are covered in paint."

"Which bit?" asked Andrei.

"Any will do."

"Then," said Andrei, "I'll start from the part I'm reading myself. I can just sketch in what comes before—first he writes about what he sees through the window, and then he begins to describe the people who make it difficult for him to stand at the window—he gives a very long and bitter list of different types."

Andrei took the booklet out of his pocket, opened it at the bookmark and began to read aloud.

"Where are they all going? What for? Do they

never hear the rhythm of the wheels or see the bare plains outside the windows? They know everything there is to know about this life, but they still just move on along the corridor, from the toilet to their compartment, from the lobby to the restaurant, gradually transforming today into one more yesterday, and they think that a God exists who will reward them or punish them for it. But if they don't go insane, it must mean they all know some secret—or else I know a secret which it would be better for no one to know. Something which makes it impossible for me ever again to walk home so innocently and senselessly, with my eyes blank and empty, along the gently swaying corridor, and not even be conscious of the fact that it is me walking along the corridor. But I don't know any secret. I simply see life as it really is, soberly and accurately, and I can never mistake this yellow catafalque rattling over the joints in the rails for anything else. I like India, and that's why I'm riding through India just at the moment. But they are simply the mad passengers of a mad train, and all I hear in the words they speak is the clattering of the wheels. And the fact that there are many of them, and I am almost alone, changes nothing. . . ."

Andrei heard a rustling sound, and looking up he saw Anton's wife putting on her boots. Anton was wiping his hands on a paint-stained rag.

"Sorry, old man," he said, "we're going to the theater. Read us the very last line, so we know how it all ends."

Andrei hesitated, then he opened the last page and read:

"Mercy is unbounded, and I know for certain that when the train stops, waiting for me there outside the yellow door will be a white elephant, on which I shall continue my eternal journey back to the Nameless."

"I get it," said Anton. "It's interesting, of course. But I don't think I'll read it all the same, thanks."

"Didn't you like it?"

"I wouldn't say I either liked it or I didn't," answered Anton. "It just has nothing to do with me personally."

"Why? What about the things you paint?" said Andrei, nodding in the direction of the painted cans. "Aren't they the same things in a different language? Stop the car, and so on? Or are you not serious about it all? Not sincere?"

"What does that mean—not serious or not sincere?" asked Anton. "Childish ideas you seem to have. Life, now, and art—creative work—are not the same. There's soc-art and conceptualism, there's modernism and postmodernism. I long since stopped confusing them with life out there. I've got a wife, and soon we'll have a child. That's really serious stuff, Andrei. I can paint anything I like, it's all just different cultural games. I only stop the cars now on these empty cans—I have to think about my child, and he'll be riding on in this real car here. You understand?"

He tapped the floor with his foot and pointed at the wall.

"It's time to go," said Olga, pulling aside the blanket hanging in the doorway. "We'll be late."

"What are you going to see?" asked Andrei.

"'Armored Train One-Sixteen-Five-Eleven,'" said Olga. "The production's very avant-garde."

"Whose production is it?"

"Upper Bunk Theater," Olga said. "Everything's all collective and anonymous down there, so no one knows whose any production is. But in secret I can let you know Anton painted the scenery.

Would you like to come along? You could get in there all right."

"No," said Andrei, "I'll call on Khan. I haven't been to see him for a long time."

"Yes, by the way, how is he getting on, down there?" asked Anton. "Has he discovered himself yet?"

"Yes," said Andrei, "and lots of other things too. See you."

"See you. Be sure to say hello from us to everyone down there."

"Anton," said Andrei as they turned to go, "can you hear anything?"

Anton stood still and listened.

"No," he said, "not a thing. What should I hear?"

2

A CALENDAR WITH A PICTURE OF KITTENS HAD
appeared on the door to Khan's compartment, concealing the familiar scratch. For a few moments,
Andrei struggled to grasp what had happened. He
looked around to make sure he'd got the right door,
then knocked. There was no answer.

Andrei opened the door. The compartment was
an incredible mess—the kind that only happens
when there's a funeral or a birth or you move house.
Sitting on Khan's bunk bed was a stout woman well
past her prime, whose puffy face still bore lingering
traces of its former ugliness: age had mercifully
removed her from the zone of aesthetic classifica-
tion. In front of her on the floor stood several suit-
cases and a basket covered with a shawl, which gave
out a dense odor of sausage. A tiny child's leg clad
in a white sock dangled over the edge of the upper
bunk, swaying gently in time with the movement of
the car.

74

"Hello," said Andrei.

"How do you do," replied the woman, looking up at him blankly.

"Where's Khan?"

"There's no one here by that name."

"You mean he's moved?"

"I don't know," she said, "maybe he's moved, or maybe he's died. We don't know. We were on the list and we got the space. Ask the conductor, he knows."

"What about his things?" asked Andrei. "Was there anything left?"

"There weren't any things here," said the woman in a livelier voice. "Don't you go getting any ideas. There weren't any things."

"Don't worry," said Andrei, "I'm not accusing you of anything. I'm just asking."

"Nothing but an empty bunk," said the woman. "And the upper bunk was empty too. I wouldn't touch anybody else's things."

"I understand," said Andrei. He turned and pushed the door open.

"You're not Andrei, are you?" the woman suddenly asked.

"Yes. Why?"

"There was a letter lying around here addressed to Andrei, but it didn't say which Andrei. Maybe it's for you."

"It is," said Andrei. "Can you give me it?"

"It was somewhere around here," the woman mumbled, rummaging through the heap of clothes on the table. "It'll take months to sort all this out. Life's awful nowadays. Always a crush in the corridor—it's too much to cope with. Found it. There it is. Are you sure it's for you? Have you got your ticket with you?"

"Haven't got one," Andrei joked familiarly.

The woman giggled, and held out the envelope.

"Save your dirty jokes for the young girls," she said skittishly. "That's all. There wasn't anything else."

"Thank you," said Andrei, putting the letter in his pocket. "Thank you very much."

"Goodbye," said the woman.

As he left the compartment, Andrei almost collided with the conductor walking along the car, but he didn't bother to ask him about Khan.

• • •

Petr Sergeievich was drunk and happy. The bottle on the table in front of him was not the usual "Railroad Special," but a fancy cut-glass bottle of "Blaze Away" cognac, with a locomotive firebox on the label. Beside it lay some drawings and blueprints—Andrei noticed that one of them showed the handle of a door lock, greatly enlarged. There were also some official-looking papers with stamps—to judge from the greasy marks on them, they must have been wrapped around the salami that Petr Sergeievich had already savaged, the tattered remnants of which were scattered around the table as if they'd been pecked by an eagle.

"How are things?"

"Okay," answered Andrei. "How are you doing?"

Petr Sergeievich raised a large hairy finger.

"Tomorrow I'll be gone all day," he said, "from early in the morning. And I won't be back at night. Will you get my sheets for me?"

"All right," said Andrei. "Just be sure to let the conductor know. Is it the thirtieth already?"

"Yes," said Petr Sergeievich, "time flies. Life could just pass you by. Have a drink?"

Andrei shook his head. He took off his shoes

and lay down on his bunk bed, turned to face the wall and took *A Guide to the Railways of India* out of his pocket. The letter was stuck between the pages. He hesitated for a moment, then stuffed the letter back into his pocket, leaving it until tomorrow. He opened the book at random.

"In essence, happiness does not exist, there is only the consciousness of happiness. Or, in other words, there is only consciousness. There is no India, no train and no window. There is only consciousness, and everything else, including ourselves, exists only in so far as it comes within its sphere. Why then, I wonder over and over again, why do we not move directly to an infinite and inexpressible happiness, abandoning everything else? Of course, we would also have to abandon ourselves. But who does the abandoning? Who is it that will be happy? And who is unhappy now?"

Andrei felt sleepy, and he found it hard to follow the words—they kept tumbling over each other as he looked at them, forming themselves into complicated geometrical tangles. He closed the book.

"Come on, Andrei," said Petr Sergeievich. "What's eating you? Have a gargle."

"I really don't feel like it, thanks," said Andrei.

"Suit yourself."

Andrei turned over onto his back and studied the dull yellow lampshade attached to the ceiling.

"Petr Sergeievich," he said. "Did you ever think about where we're going?"

"What's the problem?" Petr Sergeievich asked through a mouthful of food. "Got girl trouble? No sweat. Dump one, pick one up. Down there in the general carriages. Takes your mind off all that stuff. Know how many of the little bitches there are, out there? Money's all it takes."

"All the same, where do you think we're going?"

"You mean you don't know?"

"Why don't you just tell me?"

"No reason."

"Then tell me. Where do you think we're going?"

"Where to, where to . . . Haven't you heard it all before? Everyone knows where to, where to. Toward a ruined bridge. Andrei, why fill your fucking head with all that crap?"

1

IT WAS A CLOUDY MORNING—THE SKY OVER-
head had been replaced by a smooth grey surface
like the ceiling in the corridor, but with no ventilation pipes. Petr Sergeievich had already left. A note
for the conductor lay on the table beside two glasses
of tea that had gone cold. Andrei got dressed, took
the letter out of his pocket and immediately put it
back again. Then he locked the door and sat on the
table. Petr Sergeievich couldn't stand this, and he
would never have forgiven anyone for putting their
feet on his bunk, but there was no need to worry
about him today.

Andrei never missed a chance to spend a couple
of hours alone by the window in the compartment.
It was quite different from standing by the window
in the corridor, where you constantly had to move
to let people past and you had to interact with other
people in all sorts of other indefinable ways. Andrei
didn't really believe the author of the *Guide* when

he wrote that you could devote yourself to serene contemplation of the landscape beside the doorway of a lobby crowded with people who were yelling and shouting.

It was not a very good day—an endless wall of trees was rushing by just a few yards outside the window. Such plantations usually obscured the view for several hours, or even days, and all you could do was watch the strip of grass between the train and the trees, and examine the items thrown out from the cars of the "Yellow Arrow" that had already passed by this way.

At first everything down below was fused into one long grey-green blur, but after a few minutes his eyes adapted, so it only took a split second to identify the foreign bodies in the landscape. Perhaps it wasn't his eyes that adapted, but his imagination—he didn't so much perceive the objects rushing past the window as reconceive and recreate what must be there, on the basis of the slightest hints offered by the outside world. Anyway, there could be no mistake concerning the majority of the objects lying on the slopes of the embankment.

The commonest, of course, were the empty bottles. In the winter they were bright green spots against the snow, but now he could only distinguish them from the grass by the way they glinted. The lighter beer cans were pulled in by the slipstream, so they didn't usually travel out far from the carriages. Occasionally there were rather strange objects—in one small bog, for instance, there was a picture in an immense gold frame sticking up out of the mud. And then, about half a mile after the picture, he glimpsed the remains of a nickel-plated samovar that had smashed to pieces when it fell. Close by lay a magnificent leather suitcase, with a large fat crow standing on it. The bright white spots of used condoms were everywhere—sometimes you could confuse one with a small bone like a collarbone—and there were almost as many bones lying in the grass as bottles. Skulls were particularly numerous, probably because they were too heavy for the small rodents, and larger animals were afraid to come too close to the rumbling yellow wall. A few really old skulls had been polished a chalky white by the wind and rain, but the newer ones still had hair and pieces of flesh attached to them. Andrei was particularly amused by one skull wearing a gleam-

ing eyeglass frame, which seemed still to have
lenses in it.

The bushes and trees were littered with the
traces of recent funerals—towels of various colors,
blankets and pillow cases. They fluttered in the
wind like flags, saluting the new life rushing past
and onward; Andrei thought he remembered some
poet had said that—afterward he'd thrown himself
head-first out the window of the restaurant-car.
There were plenty of pillows too, and by no means
all new—some of them had already begun to rot in
the frequent rain of that summer. Their owners
usually lay close by, in the most varied poses and
stages of decomposition: many of them had re-
tained a dignified appearance even out on the embankment, their legs drawn up, one hand under
their head, and the other arm stretched out along
their body. There was a simple reason for this:
sometimes, at the relatives' request, the porters
would use string to tie the limbs of the deceased in
some special pose, so that they looked decorous
even in death—and it had something to do with
religion too.

Andrei noticed there were more and more white

flowers appearing in the grass by the embankment. At first he mistook them for condoms. Then he thought they were simply old flowers, until he saw that many of them were actually wrapped in cellophane, and lying with their stems upward. Eventually bouquets began to appear, and then wreaths, all made of faded white roses. Andrei guessed what it all meant: about two weeks ago they'd shown the funeral of the American pop star Isis Schopenhauer on television (her real name, Andrei remembered, was Janet Midgely). It said in the newspapers that during the ceremony two tons of the finest white roses were thrown out of the windows—the dead woman had loved white roses more than anything else in the world. They were what Andrei could see as he pressed his face against the glass. For two or three minutes more the white spots on the grass grew thicker and thicker, and then he saw a marble slab flanked by steel sphinxes, lying in the grass. Fastened on to it with gold chains was poor Isis, already well bloated in the heat. The edges of the slab were covered with advertisements—"Rolex," "Coca-Cola" and something in smaller script—it looked like the trade mark of a firm that produced vegeburgers with the "real American taste." There were two small dogs sniffing around the slab; one of them raised his muzzle towards the train and barked soundlessly. The other swiveled his tail: a long strip of something bluish-red was dangling from his jaws.

"World culture takes a long time to reach us," thought Andrei.

In the evening, just as it was beginning to get dark, the wall of trees outside the window came to an end. At first they thinned out, then gaps appeared between them, and suddenly there was an open field with a road running across it. Several brick houses stood beside the road, their windows gaping black holes and their shutters wide open. In the distance an incredibly beautiful white church with a crooked cross drifted by like a hand raised to heaven—only the upper part was visible, the rest was hidden by the forest.

Then there was a long deserted platform— Andrei spotted an old set of false teeth lying in solitary isolation on the flat concrete. Close by was a pole bearing an empty steel rectangle, which had once held a board with the name of the station. A wall made of several concrete slabs flashed by, with a tall heap of rusty iron lattices towering up behind it, then everything was hidden once again behind a dense living wall of trees—those who believed in the abominable snowmen said they had planted these trees to prevent the eyes and minds of the passengers from penetrating too far into their world.

Someone knocked on the door, and Andrei jumped up from the table.

"Who is it?" he asked.

"Abel," said a bass voice. "Come on out here, they're giving out the sheets."

When Andrei finally made up his mind to open the letter, it was already dark, and the wall of trees was still drifting by outside. He turned away from the window, took the envelope out of his pocket, and tore off the edge. Inside was a carefully torn piece of graph paper, with several lines neatly written in ink:

"Is the past history of locomotion pulled on into the future? The past always used to be someone else's or your own. Looking backwards, things seem to have disappeared from sight. Where is the key held, and who can you show it to? The pounding wheels write our journey's story. The postscript is the squeaking of the door."

The letter wasn't signed. Andrei read it through again, turned it over in his hands, folded it and slipped it back into the envelope. Then he lay down on his bunk bed, switched off the lamp above his pillow, and turned his face to the wall.

o

SOMETHING STRANGE WAS HAPPENING OUTSIDE the window, something Andrei had never seen before. The train was moving across an overpass separated by a low iron fence from the streets of a city. Outside, there were countless lights—streetlamps, the windows of houses, car headlights. But the strangest thing of all was that down below there were people, lots and lots of people. They were standing by the fence of the overpass, and when Andrei's window drifted past them, they began waving and shouting merrily. The city seemed to be celebrating some kind of festival—everyone he saw looked as though they hadn't a care in the world.

Andrei eventually began to feel oppressed by the weight of so many gazing eyes. He stood up and went out into the corridor. Outside the window on the other side of the carriage there was the usual unbroken wall of dark trees, and Andrei felt more comfortable. The corridor looked strange, some-how—the floor was covered with a thick layer of dust, the doors of all the compartments were wide open, and he could see the naked iron frames of the bunk beds. At first Andrei was surprised and even frightened, but then he remembered that apart from him, there wasn't a single other soul on the train, and he felt calmer.

He wanted to read the letter again, and he drew the folded envelope out of his pocket. As he looked over it this time, the text seemed to acquire a different sense, one which he had not seen before:

"The past is the locomotive that pulls the future after it—

Sometimes this past might even not be your own—

You are traveling backwards and see only what has already disappeared—

In order to get off the train, you need a ticket—
You hold it in your hands, but who will you show
it to?"

As he glanced over the neatly written lines,
Andrei turned back to the door of his own compartment and put his hand on the handle of the lock.
Suddenly he noticed a postscript at the very bottom
of the page, a brief note in small writing that he
hadn't spotted before—probably because it was below the fold in the paper.

At this very moment he realized he wasn't standing in the empty corridor, but lying on his bunk bed
and dreaming. He began to wake up, but in that
imperceptible instant it took to awaken, he managed to read and remember the postscript, or
rather, remember the words—in his dream they
had some quite different meaning, which could not
be forcibly dragged into the ordinary world, but
which he had just enough time to grasp:

"P.S. The problem is that we are constantly set-
ting out on a journey which is over a second before
we get started."

Andrei switched on the lamp above his pillow,
took out the letter and read it—there was no postscript at all. The place on the paper where he had

seen the postscript in his dream was only marked by
a few faint scratches, as though someone had tried
to write on it with a dried-out nib.

Something was wrong. Something had happened while he was asleep. Andrei got up from the
bunk bed and shook his head, then suddenly realized that he was surrounded by a deafening silence.
The wheels were no longer beating out their
rhythm. He looked out, and in the square of light
falling from the window he saw a motionless branch
covered in large black leaves. The train was standing still.

When Andrei went out into the corridor, everything
was the same as usual—the lights were on, there
was a smell of tobacco. But the floor under his feet
was not moving at all, and Andrei noticed he was
swaying slightly as he walked along it. The door of
the service compartment was open. Andrei glanced
in and met the gaze of the conductor, who was
standing motionless by the table, holding a glass of
tea. Andrei opened his mouth to ask what had happened to the train, but then he realized the conductor couldn't see him. At first Andrei thought he was
asleep, or he'd fallen into some kind of stupor, but

then he looked at the glass in the conductor's hand and saw the piece of sugar suspended in the tea, and the motionless string of bubbles suspended above it.

He already knew what he had to do next. He strode over to the conductor, carefully thrust his hand into the hip pocket of his jacket, and took out the key.

He stepped out into the lobby, went over to the door and put the key in the round keyhole. It didn't go in very far, because the hole was stuffed with all sorts of rubbish. He turned it. The door creaked open, and the hard dried cigarette butts crammed into the cracks around it tumbled out. Andrei thought for a moment about going back to the compartment to collect his things, but then he realized that none of the things he'd left in the suitcase under the bunk bed would be any use to him now. He stood on the edge of the ribbed iron step and stared into the boundless quiet darkness, out of which a warm wind bore a multitude of unfamiliar smells. Then he jumped down onto the embankment.

As soon as his feet hit the gravel that covered the sleepers, there was a hiss of compressed air behind him, and a second later the couplings between the carriages clanked as they stretched. The train set off and began slowly picking up speed. Andrei moved away a few yards and looked at the "Yellow Arrow."

From outside it really did look like a flying arrow of bright electric lights, fired by an unknown archer at an unknown target. Andrei looked at the point where the cars appeared, and then at the point where they disappeared; on both sides everything was blank and dark.

He turned and walked away, not really thinking about where he was going. Soon he found himself walking on an asphalt road across an open meadow, and a band of bright sky appeared on the horizon. The rumbling of the wheels behind his back gradually faded, and soon he could hear quite clearly sounds he'd never heard before—a dry chirping in the grass, the sighing of the wind and his own quiet steps.

Moscow, 1993